For Joe and Jane Artabasy, two of the good ones.—A.C.

For Stanley.—E.S.

Text copyright © 1992 by Andrew Clements.

Illustrations copyright © 1992 by Elivia Savadier.

Published by Picture Book Studio, Saxonville, Massachusetts.

Distributed in the United States by Simon & Schuster.

Distributed in Canada by Vanwell Publishing, St. Catharines, Ontario.

Library of Congress Cataloging-in-Publication Data

Clements, Andrew, 1949-

Billy and the bad teacher / written by Andrew Clements ;

illustrated by Elivia Savadier.

p. cm.

Summary: Billy makes lists of the things he dislikes about his teacher,

but when he starts to think about what his new teacher should be like

he makes an interesting discovery.

ISBN 0-88708-244-0 : $14.95

[1. Teachers—Fiction.] I. Savadier , Elivia, ill. II. Title.

PZ7.C59118Bi 1992

[E]—dc20   92-6619

CIP

AC

Ask your bookseller for these other Picture Book Studio books by Andrew Clements:

Big Al illustrated by Yoshi

Mother Earth's Counting Book illustrated by Lonni Sue Johnson

Noah & the Ark & the Animals illustrated by Ivan Gantschev

Santa's Secret Helper illustrated by Debrah Santini

Billy & The Bad Teacher

Andrew
Clements

Elivia
Savadier

Picture Book Studio

Billy was just about as perfect
as any kid in fourth grade could be.

He always did all his work neatly.
He always kept his desk and notebook very, very tidy.
He always obeyed all the rules.
And he was always on time for everything.

But Billy had trouble with his teacher.
Mr. Adams did just about everything wrong,
just about all the time. It drove Billy crazy.

So Billy did what he always did whenever
he needed to work on a problem:
He made a list.

Mr. Adams teased Mrs. Bates
about her bulletin boards.
It went on Billy's list.

Mr. Adams chewed bubble gum when
he thought no one was watching.
But Billy was watching, and he wrote it down.

Mr. Adams laughed
way too loud during
the student play.
Billy was there,
listening and writing.

When Mr. Adams was late, he ran in the halls. Out came Billy's list.

When Mr. Adams didn't eat all his lunch, Billy wrote it down.

And when Mr. Adams took a little nap at a teacher's meeting late one afternoon, only one person saw him snoozing, and that one person wrote it down on a list.

After two weeks it was a long list,
and Billy made four copies:

one for the Principal;

one for the Mayor;

one for the Governor;

and one for
the President of the United States.

He wrote four short letters,
and put the four long lists
and the four short letters
into four big envelopes.

Billy was not going to have
any more trouble
with Mr. Adams.

Billy was ready to go the post office
when he thought of a new problem:
What would his new teacher be like?
What *should* his new teacher be like?

So Billy did what he always did whenever
he needed to work on a problem:
He made a list.

The new teacher should do a handstand
on top of the big dictionary
when all the kids get 100
on their spelling tests.

The new teacher should read aloud from *The Swiss Family Robinson* every single day until it's all finished.

The new teacher should know how to make fractions and long division really fun.

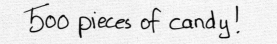

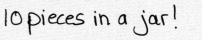

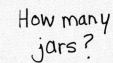

The new teacher should let the kids have some time
every day after lunch to think and write about anything at all.

The new list went on,
and when Billy stopped writing,
he read it over.

And when he read it over
he figured something out:
Most of the things on the new list
were things that Mr. Adams already did.

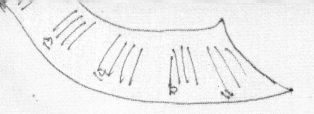

So Billy tore up the list for the Principal,
and the list for the Mayor,
and the list for the Governor,
and the list for the President of the United States...

And he decided to let Mr. Adams stay
and be his teacher anyway.